This book belongs to

_____

Paisley the Potato
Learns to Play Pickleball

Written by Rhonda Newton
Illustrated by Rhonda Newton.

Graphics by Rhonda Newton
and Anastasiya Klempach

This book is dedicated to my pickleball fanatical friend, "My Debbie Martin".

Rhonda Newton
R&R Publishing, LLC
Rathdrum, Idaho
rrpublishingllc@outlook.com
Visit the author's website at www.rrpublishingllc.com

Softcover ISBN 978-1-961847-08-8
Hardcover ISBN 978-1-961847-11-8

Paisley the Potato
Learns to Play Pickleball

Paisley the Potato was looking
for something fun to do.

She tried surfing and skiing
and had even gone to the zoo.

She reached out to her friends
to see what they were doing for fun.

They told her about a game they could
play outside in the bright, warm sun.

Paisley's friends invited her to join them and said, "You'll have a hoot!"

"Come meet us tomorrow afternoon at The Dink Institute."

Before Paisley could meet her friends,
she needed to go to the mall

to buy a sporty pickleball paddle
and a bright yellow whiffle ball.

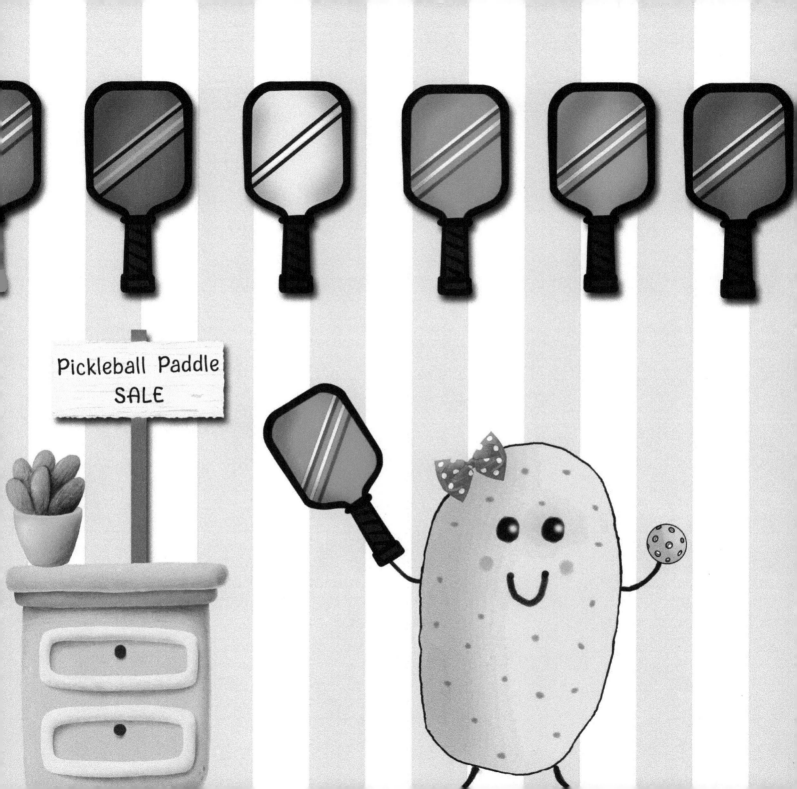

Paisley couldn't wait to meet her friends.
She knew she would have lots of fun.

She was looking forward to breathing in
the fresh air outside in the bright, warm sun.

Paisley learned how to keep score,
whether for two players or four.

She figured out the best way to play
well, was to simply hit the ball more.

She studied and practiced in her spare time
with high hopes one day she would win.

Her hard work was paying off big.
In no time she had perfected her backspin!

Paisley was having a lot of fun but
her eyes were itching more and more.

She could tell she wasn't playing
well due to her eyes feeling so very sore.

Paisley tried with all her might
to stop her eyes from twitching.

She was worried that if her vision was blurry,
she would end up stepping into "the kitchen".

Players should avoid stepping foot in the non-volley zone, also known as "the kitchen".

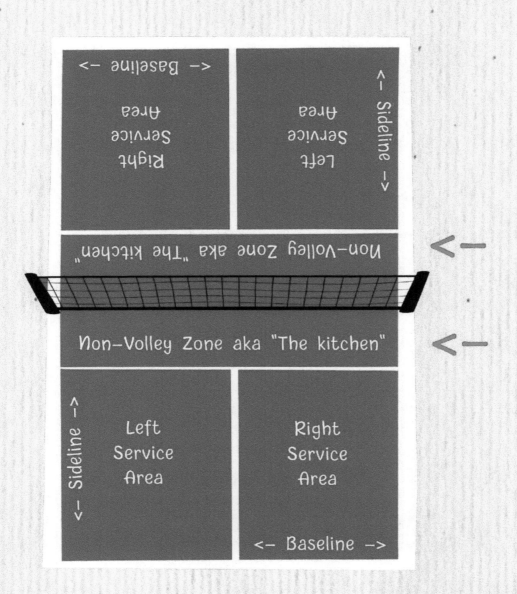

Paisley was about to start a tournament
but as her first game was about to begin,

she noticed the trees around her were
swaying back and forth in the wind.

Paisley couldn't see anything in front of her face from the pollen blowing off the trees.

There was so much floating around in the sky, it brought Paisley right down to her knees.

Paisley's eyes continued to water
and she was having to gasp for air.

Her head was starting to hurt pretty bad
from the thick air and the sun's bright glare.

By the time her tournament was over,
Paisley was feeling a little sad.

Despite trying her hardest to do well,
she knew she had played pretty bad.

Paisley was hoping to become a professional player.
She was a pro at hitting the ball!

But she decided she needed to take a long break.
She would do much better playing pickleball in the fall.

Printed in the USA
CPSIA information can be obtained
at www.ICGtesting.com
CBHW062201021224
18346CB00022B/1440